The Little Dyslexic Angel

Special Christmas Edition

Written and Illustrated by
ROBERT WARRINGTON

Edited by
C. E. Moore

Gazebo Books may be purchased through booksellers or by going to www.GazeboBooksPublishing.com

Copyright 2008 and 2011. All rights reserved.

www.LittleDyslexicAngel.com

ISBN: 978-0-984-47483-7 (hardcover)
ISBN: 978-0-984-47484-4 (paperback)
ISBN: 978-0-984-47485-1 (e-book)

Library of Congress Control Number: 2011960809

Printed in the United States of America.

Inspired by and dedicated to

my littlest angel, Kelli,
and her sisters, Krysten and Kelsey,
and Sam and Jake,
all voices in my choir of angels.

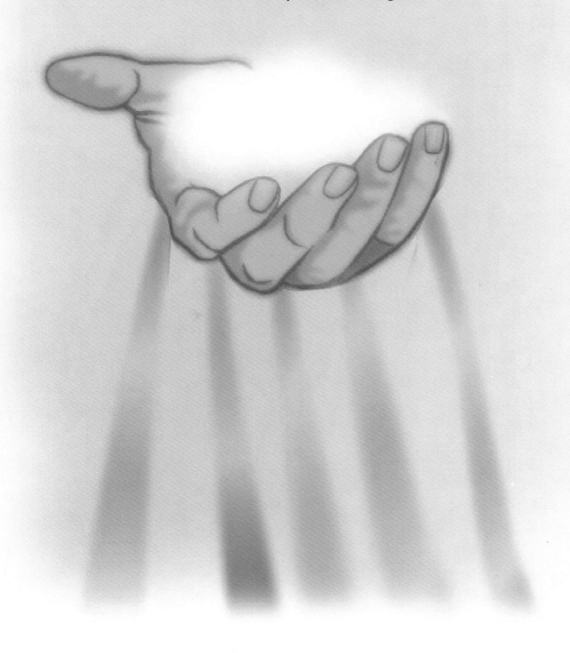

Foreword

Hope and Dreams

Hold on to hope for if it is lost,
life's like a canyon impossible to cross.
Hold on to dreams, forever more;
your hopes and dreams will help you soar.

by S. C. Moore

She rose up out of a wave.
That was her first memory.

Not just any wave, a great tidal wave.
It was so vast it swept across the whole
of Indonesia, on the day after Christmas,
devastating everything and everyone in its path.

She was an angel, an angel created
from all the hopes and dreams
of the sweet young souls
the wave swept off
to Heaven.

After the wave receded,
she floated on a cloud
above the land.

As the souls
of the children
drifted by her on
their way to Heaven,
they shared their
hopes and dreams,
and the little angel
grew stronger.

When she had said goodbye to the
last young soul the wave had taken,
the little angel floated alone,
overflowing with hopes and dreams.

God placed the souls of the children
in His heavenly choir, and she could
hear their sweet voices singing.
Then, God spoke to her.

"You are my new angel, the first one I have created in a thousand years.
You are my angel of the innocent. The world has gone mad and grown
dangerous. The innocent children on Earth need your help and
guidance so their hopes and dreams may someday become real."

"Thank you, Great Father." The little angel smiled, warmed
by his voice. "I can't wait to get to Heaven and begin my work."

"You must wait, my little angel, for first you must find your name."

"Don't you give me my name, Great Father?" the newest little angel asked.

"Oh, you have a name, my dear, but you must read your name and learn your own special lesson. I have written them on the wind and hidden them in the rainbows."

"Why can't you tell me now? I really want to fly up to Heaven and be with you. I want to see all the sweet children that shared their hopes and dreams with me."

"So you shall, my child. But first, you must know who you are. You can only learn that by yourself. Once you know, you can become all that you hope and dream you will be, just like the little children's hopes and dreams that formed you."

"If you tell me now, I'll know it." The little angel blinked in confusion.

"No, my child. If I tell you, it will only be something you heard. It must be something you feel with every hope and dream that made you. Then your wings will grow, spread wide and strong, and carry you to Heaven. Until then, you must float on your cloud and seek your name and your lesson hidden in the rainbows."

"I'd much rather go to Heaven with you now," the little angel told God sweetly and flashed a dazzling smile.

"No, dear one," God laughed. "Life for an angel is no simpler than life for a child. You must learn your lesson before you can fly. You must do this for the children so you know what all their hopes and dreams really meant to them."

"I would do anything for the children and for you, Great Father."

"Then I will see you in Heaven when you know your name and have learned your lesson. Until then, listen to the hopes and dreams of the children on Earth, and hold them in your heart."

With that, the voice of God was gone, and the little angel
was alone, floating on the wind.

It was not long before a winged angel flew by on her way from
Heaven to Earth, and declared, "Hello, my name is Serenity."
She had ebony skin, hazel brown eyes, and deep, rich, reddish-
brown hair piled high upon her head.

"Hello, Serenity!" the little angel cried, delighted to meet
one of God's winged angels.

"My, what a beautiful little angel you are," Serenity told her.
"What is your name?"

"I don't know yet," replied the little angel. "God has written my
name and my lesson on the wind and hidden them in the rainbows.
I need to find them, but I must float, and the only rainbow I see
is so very far away."

"I can fly," Serenity told her with pride. "You're so sweet.
It would be lovely to have you in Heaven with us. I'll fly you
to the rainbow so you can read your name and learn your lesson."

"That would be marvelous!" exclaimed the little angel.

So, Serenity pushed her little cloud and flew them
to the nearest rainbow.

"Oh my," the little angel gasped. "I didn't know
a rainbow would be so beautiful!"

Serenity smiled at her.
"Is this your first rainbow?"

Goals to achieve
Dreams are just
That saves
to
Dreams
to achieve
Faith
are just

"Yes it is," giggled the
little angel. "It almost
makes me dizzy with
all its colors. What are
all those dots, lines, and
curves floating in the rainbow?"

"Why, those
are not dots,
lines, and curves,
little angel."

"Those are the words God
wrote on the wind so you
may read your name
and learn your lesson,"
Serenity explained.

"Oh, how fabulous! But
I'm afraid they don't
make any sense to me."

"Well," Serenity said
thoughtfully, "perhaps you
really are a bit dizzy from all
the colors. After all, this is
your first rainbow, and that
can be very overwhelming.

I must fly to Earth now, little angel,
and give the children my gift of serenity.
Then they may learn to accept their place
in God's plan and live their lives with peace
in their hearts."

"Oh, don't worry about me,"
the little angel told her.

"Of course I won't," laughed Serenity.
"You are the newest little angel and
part of God's plan. I'm sure your
dizziness will pass once you're calm.
When you've read your name and
learned your lesson, you can fly
to Heaven and see me again."

"That would be wonderful!"
the little angel beamed.
Then she waved good-bye
to Serenity as she flew
down to Earth.

She turned to look again at the rainbow filled with dots, lines, and curves that spelled out her name and her lesson. She squinted, trying to make the letters stand still so she could read them. The little angel looked and looked at them until the rainbow finally faded, but she was unable to read her name or her lesson.

"I did what I was told. Why can't I read my own name?"
she cried. "Is something wrong with me?"

Then the little angel remembered Serenity's words. She realized
all things come with time, and everything is part of God's plan.
Maybe she just needed to find a few more rainbows and try a few
more times before she could read her name and learn her lesson.

The little angel floated calmly onward through the sky. She didn't know how long she had been drifting, listening to the hopes and dreams of the sleeping children below, for time passes differently for angels. It was quite some time, though, before another angel saw her and flew over to greet her.

"Hello, my name is Courage. You must be the new little angel Serenity told me about. Have you read your name and learned your lesson yet?"

"No, not yet," sighed the little angel, "but it's been a long time since I floated through a rainbow."

"Well, then," Courage flashed a dazzling, white smile beneath his wavy, lush, dark brown hair, "let's go find one together so you can grow your wings."

His strong, copper-colored hand clasped her tiny hand gently. Courage flew her straight to the biggest, brightest rainbow he could see, and angels can see very, very far.

"There!" pointed Courage. "I can see your name, and your lesson stretches all across the rainbow and back again."

"Oh, my goodness! What is my name?" cried the little angel with joy.

"It's right there," Courage frowned, pointing out God's words glowing against the rainbow.

"But those are just a bunch of dots, lines, and curves," the little angel frowned back at him. "Can't you tell me my name, please?"

"You must read your name for yourself.
It is forbidden for anyone to tell you.
Those dots, lines, and curves
are what spell your name
and your lesson. Can't
you read your
words from
God?"

"I see them, but
I can't understand
what they say," and
the little angel sulked.

"Well, you are very young,"
Courage considered.

"It seems like I've been
floating in the sky forever.
I'm afraid I'll never learn
to read the words God
has written on the
rainbows for me,"
she said tearfully.

"You are an angel." Courage gently patted her hand. "You have all the strength you need to see you through this. Perhaps you're meant to hear more hopes and dreams before you'll be able to read your name and learn your lesson," he said kindly.

"Perhaps you're right," sighed the little angel.

"I'll leave you here by the rainbow. I must go to Earth and give courage to all the children to help them change the things they can."

"Then you mustn't worry about me. Hurry down to the children and give them all the courage they need," she insisted.

"Be determined, and don't give up," Courage consoled her,
"and before you know it, I'll see you in Heaven."

Then, the valiant angel soared
down to Earth. The little angel
watched him fly with his great,
white wings until he was just
a tiny speck of dazzling light.

She smiled and confidently returned
to listening to hopes and dreams.
She now understood how important
it was for children to have courage
to deal with trouble in their lives.

The rainbow slowly faded and the little angel was once again alone
in the big open sky. She floated along, hearing all sorts of hopes
and dreams, until she drifted into another rainbow. She saw what
must be her name and her lesson, but none of the words made sense.
They were all nothing more than dots, lines, and curves.

The little angel looked and looked at the rainbow for as long and as hard as she could until it slowly faded away. Sadly, she still was not able to read her name or learn her lesson.

"Oh my," she cried, in a sad way, not a glad way.
"What's wrong with me?"

The little angel traveled on for
some time before she arrived
at another rainbow.

Suddenly, she heard the sound of rustling wings,
and there was another angel floating beside her.
This one was beautiful in a totally different way.
She had exquisite, dark, almond-shaped eyes and
skin like golden-colored sunlight.

"What's the matter, little angel?
Why are you so sad?"

"I'm trying to read my name and learn my lesson that God
has written on the wind and hidden in the rainbows. I can
see what He wrote, but I don't understand the words at all."

"You can't read them?" the lovely
angel asked. "They're right there
in the colors of the rainbow."

"No!" shouted the little angel. This
time she cried with tears in her eyes
and not with the sound of her voice.
"I just see dots, lines, and curves."

"Don't worry, little angel. My name is Wisdom. Many people, young and old, can't see what's right in front of them because they don't look at it correctly. We all learn in different ways, and you must find the way which is best for you. Be persistent, and keep trying to see a meaning in the dots, lines, and curves, and everything will be alright." Wisdom smiled, and her long, black hair wafted on the wind beneath her halo.

"You carry the word of God inside you. That's what makes you an angel. His word will guide you on your journey."

With a flash of her dazzling smile,
she spun around on her giant,
downy wings and sped
toward Earth.

"Wisdom is right! I know
the word of God," she laughed.
"The word of God is *love*,"
the little angel sang out.
"Goodbye, Wisdom!" she cried
as she waved thankfully.

Once again the little angel was alone in the sky.
She floated along, listening to more hopes and dreams
for a very, very long time. More angels waved at her
as they passed by, but they didn't stop to visit with her.

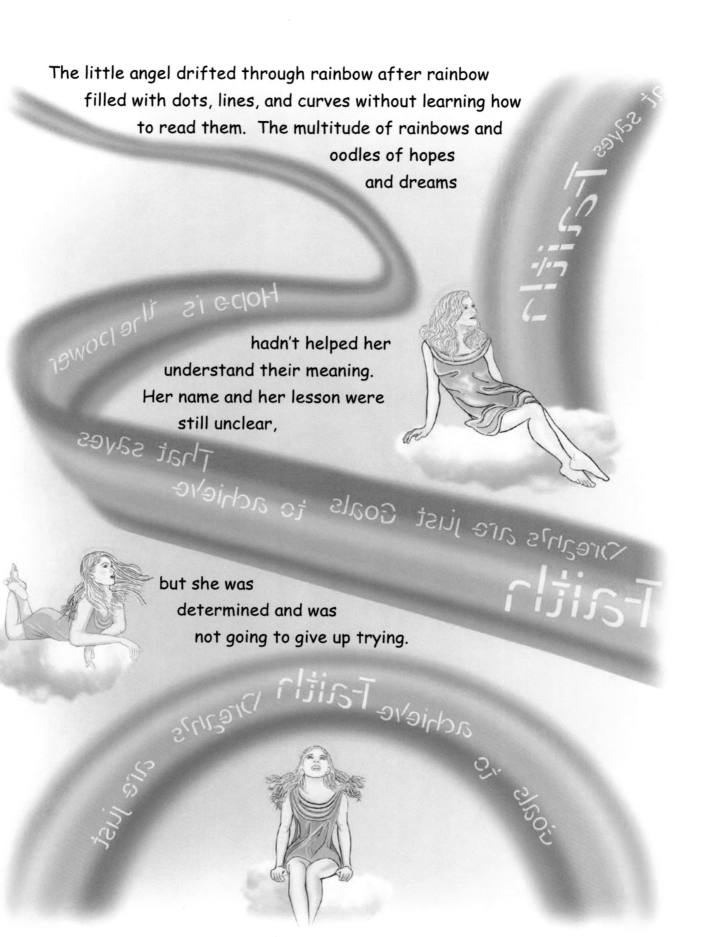

The little angel drifted through rainbow after rainbow
filled with dots, lines, and curves without learning how
to read them. The multitude of rainbows and
oodles of hopes
and dreams

hadn't helped her
understand their meaning.
Her name and her lesson were
still unclear,

but she was
determined and was
not going to give up trying.

Although the newest little angel had not yet learned her name or her lesson, she had learned many, many other things on her long journey.

Serenity helped her learn that patience is important when facing new challenges. Courage taught her that even if you fail once, you must be brave and not give up. Wisdom helped her realize that there is more than one way to look at something, and how powerful an act of kindness can be.

She understood the power of hope and why children need their dreams. Knowing all of this made her grow brighter as she floated in the sky.

Then, one Christmas Eve, Santa saw her as he was flying his sleigh around the world delivering toys and gifts to all the good little children.

She was the first angel God had created in a thousand years, and Santa had never seen a new angel before.

"Rudolph, look up there!"
Santa pointed out the sparkling
form to his lead reindeer.
"What do you think that is?"

"I don't know, Santa,"
Rudolph replied.

"I think we have time
to find out what it is
before we deliver the rest
of these toys and goodies,"
Santa decided.

So off they flew to see what was
gleaming in the sky above them.

Santa stopped his sleigh right beside the little angel floating on her cloud. He looked at her milky white skin, her dazzling, blue eyes, and her golden hair shining as brightly as the sun. "Are you a star or an angel?" he asked.

"Santa!" she exclaimed with glee, for the little angel knew exactly who he was. Many of the children's hopes and dreams she had heard over the years had been about Santa bringing something wonderful on Christmas.

"I'm an angel, but I have not yet earned my wings.
I must read my name and learn my lesson that God
has written on the wind and hidden in the rainbows.
As soon as I do, I will grow my wings so I can
fly to Heaven."

"Haven't you floated into a rainbow yet?" Santa asked.

"I've floated into many, many rainbows. I've been trying to read
my name and learn my lesson for a very long time, but rainbows never
last long enough. They always fade and disappear before I can make
any sense of all the dots, lines, and curves I see that are His words."

"I live at the North Pole where the Aurora Borealis is," Santa told her. "It glows with the colors of a rainbow and lasts a very long time. Why don't you ride in my sleigh with me while I deliver my presents, and then you can return with me to the North Pole?"

"That would be fantastic!" cried the little angel. She floated down into Santa's sleigh and settled right beside him in front of the gigantic bag of gifts he carried.

The night seemed to fly by as fast as a shooting star as the little angel circled the world with Santa.

They laughed, talked, and sang
every Christmas carol they knew
as they flew along.

The little angel shared with Santa
some of the many, many hopes and
dreams she had heard over the years.

"Santa, how do you decide
if they are good or bad children?"
the little angel questioned.

She loved all children and never thought any of them were truly bad.

"To be good, they must care for others and be kind to everyone," Santa explained. "That's what I call a good little child."

"How do you choose what gift to give them?" the little angel asked.

"I don't always give them what they ask for," Santa winked, "I give them the gift they need."

"That is a wise and wonderful thing!" laughed the little angel.

"Yes it is," Santa laughed back at her.

On and on they flew, delivering present after present until the gigantic bag was empty. Then they headed back to the North Pole. All of a sudden, the little angel realized the sky around them was starting to glow with all the colors of the rainbows.

"We're almost home," Santa chuckled. "We're flying through the Aurora Borealis."

"Oh Santa, it's so gigantic, so incredible! I can see the words God wrote for me floating all around, but they still look like dots, lines, and curves."

"Well, many children on Earth have something called dyslexia," Santa told her.

"Is that an illness?" asked the little angel.

"Oh, no," Santa laughed. "Children with dyslexia are very healthy and very smart. Sometimes they have more trouble learning than other children do, but with hard work and determination, they can do anything.

There are many famous singers, actors, artists, athletes, scientists, and other successful people with dyslexia."

"Oh!" exclaimed the little angel.

"There are some dyslexic children who see dots, lines, and curves backwards or moving around like you do, little angel."

Santa reached into his bag, pulled out one last gift, and handed it to her. It was a beautiful golden mirror framed by a circle of winged angels.

"Oh my!" she gasped as she gently took the mirror and held it in her hands. "It's lovely! But how can a mirror help me?"

"Maybe if you look at the words God wrote for you in the reflection of the mirror, it will turn them around so you'll be able to read your name and your lesson," Santa smiled encouragingly.

Dreams are just
Goals to achieve

Faith

Hope is the power
That saves

"Really?" asked the little angel.

"Really," Santa answered.

So, the little angel took a
deep breath and held up her gift.

Dreams are just
Goals

Faith

dreams are just
Goals to achieve

Hope is the power
That saves

Hope is the power
That saves

She turned the mirror so she
could see the reflection of the
words God wrote just for her
floating in the colors of
the Aurora Borealis.

"Oh my!" cried the little angel. "The dots, lines, and curves look completely different now. I think I can read them."

"What do they say, little angel?" Santa questioned.

"My name is...Faith," she sighed with pleasure.

"That's an excellent name for you, little angel," Santa laughed, and his laugh was loud and jolly.

"My lesson says...hope is the power that saves, and ...dreams are just goals to achieve."

"And faith," Santa winked, "is the way to share your lesson."

Suddenly, the sound of heavenly voices encircled the Aurora Borealis, and the little angel felt a warm and tingly feeling swell within her shoulders.

She turned her head to look, and there on her back
was the biggest, brightest pair of wings
she had ever seen.

"Ho, ho, ho!"
chuckled Santa.

"An angel who
earns her wings
on Christmas
must be a very
special angel indeed!"
he exclaimed.

"Thank you, Santa!
Thank you so much."
She gave him a great
big hug, and then Faith
soared up toward Heaven
on her new, dazzling,
white wings.

When Faith arrived
at the Pearly Gates,
Serenity, Courage, and Wisdom
were waiting to greet her. Then
she saw the heavenly choir and
marveled at their glorious voices.

"Faith, I am very proud of you."
The voice of God spoke to her
as she settled down on a heavenly
cloud. "Although your task was
difficult, you prevailed in your
quest. You spent the time you
needed to achieve your goal. That
took serenity, courage, wisdom, and
most of all, faith. I have decided
you will be my Christmas angel
so you may share your faith with
all the little children of the world."

"That would please me very much,
Great Father," Faith replied.

So, from then on, to Faith's delight,
she flew above Santa's sleigh
every Christmas Eve.

She shared her gift
with the message
she had learned:

You must have faith
in yourself to make your
hopes and dreams come true.

The Serenity Prayer

God grant me the serenity
to accept the things I cannot change,
the courage to change the things I can,
and the wisdom to know the difference...

NOTES FROM THE PUBLISHER

Santa and the little angel flew over many, many landmarks on Christmas Eve on their journey around the world delivering presents. The landmarks pictured in this book are just a few of those, and their names and locations are provided below to allow readers to learn more about them and to promote discussions between children and their parents.

Rio de Janeiro, Brazil; the **Statue of Jesus**

Cuzco, Peru; **Machu Picchu**

Yucatán, Mexico; **Chichen Itza**

Dallas, Texas; **Bank of America Tower,**

   Fountain Place, Hunt Building, Reunion Tower

San Francisco, California; the **Golden Gate Bridge**

Cannon Beach, Oregon; **Haystack Rock**

Seattle, Washington; the **Space Needle**

New York City, New York; the **Statue of Liberty**

Copenhagen, Denmark; the **Little Mermaid**

Amesbury, England; **Stonehenge**

Paris, France; the **Eiffel Tower**

Berlin, Germany; the **Brandenburg Gate**

Pisa, Italy; the **Leaning Tower of Pisa**

Athens, Greece; the **Acropolis**

Giza, Egypt; the **Pyramids of Giza**

Agra, India; the **Taj Mahal**

Sydney, Australia; the **Sydney Opera House**

Nara, Japan; **Goju-no-to Pagoda**

Beijing, China; the **Great Wall**

Moscow, Russia; **St. Basil's Cathedral**

INFORMATION ON DYSLEXIA FROM THE PUBLISHER

Many children with learning problems go undiagnosed and face difficult challenges working within the public school system. Most teachers are untrained to work with learning/language disabilities or with children who are gifted and talented. Children with dyslexia may fall into either of these categories. They are intelligent, often above average, and they learn in different ways than their peers. Only a small percentage of children see words backwards like the little angel did. Most dyslexics have more trouble with tracking, phrasing, comprehension, and inference when learning to read. Some face more difficulty with learning math, spelling, writing, organization, or any combination of the above. Most function better with a schedule and routine, and they often need more repetition with new concepts before understanding them, especially with things like spelling and math facts. For parents, grandparents, and siblings of children with dyslexia, it is essential to be aware of these differences, and above all to be patient and supportive of a child who is struggling in school. Below is a list of reference websites which may be helpful to children with dyslexia and their families.

http://www.interdys.org

http://dyslexiamylife.org

http://www.slingerland.org

http://www.ortongillingham.com

http://www.dyslexia-parent.com/hints.html

http://www.beingdyslexic.co.uk

http://www.dyslexia-test.com/famous.html

http://www.mayoclinic.com/health/dyslexia

http://children.webmd.com/tc/dyslexia-treatment

http://www.smartkidswithld.org

http://www.ninds.nih.gov/disorders/dyslexia

FAMOUS CONTEMPORARY FIGURES WITH DYSLEXIA

Tom Cruise

Orlando Bloom

Steve Jobs

Cher

Jay Leno

Salma Hayek

Jewel

Keira Knightley

Will Smith

Patrick Dempsey

Magic Johnson

Richard Branson

Danny Glover

Woody Harrelson

Henry Winkler

Richard Ford

Whoopi Goldberg

Duncan Goodhew

Susan Hampshire

Eddie Izzard

Steve Redgrave

P!nk

Rodin Charles Schwab

Steven Spielberg

Jackie Stewart

Thomas J. Watson, Jr.

Benjamin Zephaniah

Bruce Jenner

William Hewlett

Robin Williams

Stephen J. Cannell

Ted Turner

Terry Goodkind

Greg Louganis

Keanu Reeves

Al Roker

Alyssa Milano

Liv Tyler

Lady Gaga

George Burns

Harry Belafonte

Lindsay Wagner

FAMOUS HISTORICAL FIGURES WITH DYSLEXIA

Andy Warhol

Ansel Adams

Nelson Rockefeller

Agatha Christie

John Lennon

Babe Ruth

Walt Disney

Winston Churchill

General George Patton

Gustave Flaubert

Thomas Edison

Pablo Picasso

The Wright Brothers

Charles Lindbergh

Hans Christian Andersen

Lewis Carroll

Leonardo da Vinci

Alexander Graham Bell

Thomas Jefferson

John F. Kennedy

Henry Ford

Woodrow Wilson

George Washington

Albert Einstein

Andrew Jackson

William Butler Yeats

Ludwig van Beethoven

Richard Strauss

Michelangelo

Sir Isaac Newton

Ernest Hemingway

ABOUT THE AUTHOR

Robert Warrington spent several decades living and working in New York City in the entertainment industry before relocating to the Pacific Northwest. This is Robert's first children's book. The story was inspired by his youngest niece, who struggled for years to learn to read and told him that words on a page moved around and looked like, "...dots, lines, and curves." She and her two sisters have dyslexia and faced many difficulties with learning throughout their school years.

A portion of the proceeds from this book will go to dyslexia organizations.

CPSIA information can be obtained
at www.ICGtesting.com
Printed in the USA
LVIC040837230612
287242LV00004BB